Dating a Single Minister: *A Gorgeous Fashion Mogul's Story*

By: *Eddie Johnson*

Rare Jewels Publishing Company

Books by Eddie Johnson:

Romance Church Drama Category

Temptation in the Pulpit

Dating a Single Minister

Megan's Fools Paradise

Poetry Category

Reaching For Celestial Heights

The *Love* of a Mother & Father

www.EddieJohnson.net

Copyright © 2017 Eddie Johnson

ISBN: 978-0-9827188-4-1

*Ch*apter 1

Tuesday morning, Summer Reed was in Summer's Bridal Fashions lobby when in walked the finest African American male she had ever seen. After retrieving her mail, Summer returned to her office. He stopped at the receptionist desk. "I am here to meet with Summer, kindly let her know that Derrick Hamilton is waiting."

"And who are you, Derrick Hamilton?"

"I am an architect Summer is considering hiring. She probably forgot to pencil me in for you."

Beverly buzzed Summer's phone.

"Yes Beverly."

"I have a nice looking gentleman here for you. He says that his name is Derrick Hamilton."

"He must be with Hamilton Architectural Designs. Let Mr. Hamilton know that I'll be with him in a moment."

"Okay. And for your information Summer, Derrick Hamilton is also a local single minister. Barbara and I attended a New Year's watch night service at Grace Missionary Baptist Church where Mr. Hamilton resides as the senior minister. He's quite a dynamic speaker."

Summer walked out of her office, strolled down the hall, and then back out into the lobby. He noticed Summer approaching and then stood to his feet. She walked over to him.

"You must be the lovely Summer Reed."

"Yes I am."

"Well, I am going to be your architect."

"Slow down Mr. Hamilton. Why don't you follow me back to my office?"

"Okay."

After Derrick was seated, Summer wasted no time in getting down to business. "I need to find out more about your company and your ability to help me bring to fruition a premier mega bridal boutique."

"And how would you define a mega bridal boutique." Derrick removed a digital tablet from his briefcase and began to take notes.

"It should be a one stop wedding shop," Summer responded with passion. "Not only would we carry outfits for the bridal party, we would also have floral arrangements for the wedding ceremony. A wedding planner and photographer would also be on staff. Our wedding planner will be capable of coordinating all wedding particulars including catering services. There should be several offices and meeting rooms for personnel. A section of the building should be set aside specifically for the magazine publishing arm of the company."

"Hamilton Architectural Designs have been around well over forty-five years," Derrick said. "My late father Damon Hamilton started the firm. He died while on a fishing expedition about seven years ago."

"I am sorry to hear of your loss. But it is really nice of you to carry on his legacy."

After a brief silence, Summer continued. "Not to change our focus, I hear that you are a minister."

"You heard right. At the time of dad's death I was fresh out seminary." Derrick paused. "I worked in his firm for about five years before I realized being an architect wasn't my true calling. So I shelved my architectural degree and went off to pursue a ministerial career. After completing seminary I became the Assistant Minister at Grace Missionary Baptist Church following a brief stint as an associate minister. Grace's Senior Minister Cleophus Harris was dismissed after a church scandal investigation. God bless his soul; shortly thereafter, Minister Harris passed away. I was well loved by the parishioners and was voted in as his successor." Derrick noticed Summer's eyes were locked on him. "We should put our attention back on the reason I am here. I have renderings of shops and office buildings my firm has designed over the years." He went over different drawings and highlighted how he could incorporate similar designs into her building and yet make it unique unto itself. When their meeting concluded Summer informed him that she would select an architect within a couple weeks.

"Do you think I'll have a chance of seeing you personally; even if I don't design your shop," Derrick quizzed.

"You are not married are you?"

"No. I am still a divorcee as of the last time I checked.

"Divorced! You are divorced?" Summer exclaimed.

"Yes. My beloved children's mother had a fling with her childhood sweetheart a Mr. Michael Gibbs a used car salesman while I was away at seminary. Thus we divorced. I have two high school age children. My daughter's name is Angel and my son's name is Roderick."

"My ex and I share custody of our kids."

"That is fine Mr. Hamilton."

"Just call me, Derrick."

"Well Derrick, I am going to take a rain check."

"Why?"

"I have always vowed not to date married men or divorcees."

"On a different note, I always make it habit of asking my customers or potential business partners how they learned of my firm."

"A friend of mine Jasmine Williams referred you. She seemed very knowledgeable of you and some of the projects that you've designed."

"Jasmine probably neglected to tell you of our past involvement," Derrick promptly replied. "We dated for a little over a year."

"Who Jasmine dates or dated is her own business."

"However, you're probably trying to figure out why we're no longer together. Jasmine's main drawback was that she was too jealous and overly possessive."

"That kind of behavior must have been quite stifling. A minister has to be able to interact freely with people."

"You understand me as a person. That's exactly why we should be together."

Summer flat out disagreed. "I don't date ex mates of my friends!"

"You'll need to make an exception."

"Derrick, I have a business to run. You need to be going. You probably have other work and clients just begging for your attention."

After standing to their feet, Summer extended a hand. He reached out and shook her hand.

"I look forward to our next meeting when I will finally get to be your architect."

"I'll be in touch." Summer walked Derrick out to the lobby.

*Ch*apter 2

Summer's employees awaited the start of their weekly focus meeting. Missing from the group was verbally combative and often controversial fashion consultant and materials buyer Fay Edwards. Having cut ties with Summer, she now worked for an upstart competitor Sid Edelman's Bridal Wear. Terry Springer a new hire photographer who also freelanced for Sid informed Summer rumor has it Fay divulged her company's ideas to Sid for the forthcoming New York Bridal Fashion Competition. As a result, Summer was more determined than ever to win. Having learned a tough lesson, she'd require all future employees to sign a two year non-compete agreement. But she would soon find out that Fay's defection and alleged subsequent breach of trust would only be the beginning of her hardships.

Opening up the meeting, Summer congratulated everyone for a job well done on the latest issue of their national quarterly publication. "Sales have increased exponentially due to fresh marketing channels being tapped," Summer noted. "I'd like to thank our advertising department. Revenue for

Summer's Bridal Fashions Magazine is up more than twofold over the same quarter last year." Summer straightened her podium notes. "We have a new staff member. Today is his first day. Terry Springer, please stand for a moment." He stood. Everyone rose to his or her feet for a brief moment with a rousing hand of applause. "Terry is a photographer. He will be working alongside Ted D' Francisco. The two should complement each other."

Sitting at her cluttered desk, once the meeting concluded, Summer thoughts were on the company's teen outreach program. Summer spearheaded a magazine contest in which twenty-five young women were chosen winners from entrants with an interest in fashion merchandising. Ms. Amelia Richards the top winner, a local high school senior, was awarded five thousand dollars earmarked for college tuition. All contestants winners Ms. Richards included would get to be Summer's special guest at the prestigious afore-mentioned fashion gala.

Summer grew up on the outskirts of Atlanta, Georgia. She was the younger of two siblings.

Summer's brother Bill was among the most influential and wealthiest criminal prosecuting attorneys in Southern California.

The phone rang and she answered. "Summer Reed speaking, how may I help you?"

Hello Summer. This is William Reed."

"You can spare me your rich man introduction. How is my big brother Bill?"

"I'm fine. I am calling to accept your invitation to your stellar engagement."

"That's great; I'll look forward to having my whole family together for this year's event, providing there aren't any unforeseen problems."

"What do you mean?"

"Don't worry about it," Summer's tone was happy, yet a little weary. "I intend to win the competition for the first time."

"Sounds like you will be pulling out all the stops. I can't wait to see what you have up your sleeves."

"So what's new Bill?"

"Well I have decided to expand my law firm to the East Coast. I'm opening an office in Lower Manhattan."

"Great! We'll see more of each other," Summer replied. "How are the children and Sylvia?"

"Everyone is fine. Sylvia remains the ideal preeminent wife of a high profile multi-million dollar attorney; while still managing to be a successful pediatrician, and literary scholar. And she still attends most of my elite social outings while volunteering for local charities."

"Sylvia does all of that yet devotes time for her husband and kids. That's quite a woman."

"My sentiments exactly. How is your love life?"

"It's non-existent. However, I'm determined to find someone."

"I don't see that happening. You are too devoted to your company."

"I would love to prove you wrong!" She distraughtly yelled. "You have a spouse with a successful career! Why can't I do the same?"

"Do you have any love prospects?" Bill taunted.

"A financially secure black brother recently displayed an interest in me. I turned him down. His name is Derrick Hamilton. He is a successful local architect and minister."

"My point well taken. You don't have time for an involved relationship. Why wasn't he given a chance?"

"He's a divorcee with teenage children."

"My dear sister take care. I'm due in court shortly."

*Ch*apter 3

Summer timely submitted Summer's Bridal Fashions' entry to the New York Bridal Fashions Competition Committee. A week later she received a phone call from its chairman Sasha Mills.

"The fashion committee has a concern as it relates to your entry. Sid the owner of Sid Edelman's Bridal Wear presented an identical plan to the one you subsequently submitted."

"Really. How could he have submitted my plan before I had a chance?" Summer thought to herself: *Terry Springer was right, Fay divulged my privilege information.* Summer stared Sasha directly in the eyes. "Sid and I haven't spoken in a while. My ex fashion consultant Fay Edwards must have divulged my ideas to her new employer. Everything I documented from clothing to modeling came from my own in house personnel. I have signed intents for purchases to back up my statement."

"Are you willing to file a complaint against Sid?" Sasha asked.

"I would only consider doing so if my company were in jeopardy of being disqualified."

"I'll get back to you once I discuss the matter further with my fellow committee members."

Summer took to the internet to release stress. Talking aloud while typing she set up a profile with an online dating service. "My ideal mate should be a well-educated black male who preferably has a master's degree. He should be a single monogamous heterosexual with no children. I also prefer him not to be a divorcee."

Once she finished setting up the site information, Summer contacted her best friend Brenda Jamison. "Hi Brenda. You are going to think I've lost my mind. I have stooped to the level of seeking love over the internet in search of a knight in shining armor to rescue me from my love doldrums."

"Girl, you are desperate. Maybe you should let me hook you up with one of Barry's buddies."

"No Brenda. I have seen Barry's buddies. His friends are not affluent enough to fit into my elite world."

"Even if you are right Summer, you don't have time for a man. You are married to your work."

"Everybody feels compelled to tell me the same thing. Well Ms. Brenda I have to find a man. My biological clock is ticking, and I don't want my time to run out. It would be nice to have a husband and a couple of kids. I too have a dream of living in a house with a white picket fence with a family to call my own."

Saturday morning, Derrick was working out at a local fitness gym with his brother Brad. He teased Derrick, "You have always been the lucky roller. Do you really think you can snag the boutique design contract and at the same time get its proprietor the lovely Ms. Summer Reed to be your lady?"

"She is a true professional. If I am ever to be serious with a woman then Summer could be the one."

"I have never seen you so turned on by thought of a woman," Brad said.

"I can tell by the look in her eyes that she is hot for me," Derrick replied. If I am persistent in my pursuit of Summer, I will win her over."

Three women scantily clad in workout attire enamored by Derrick and his brother's muscular chiseled physiques strolled by as he finished his remark. Camilla was the out spoken member of the three. "Hi Guys. Don't let us girls interrupt your work out," she gingerly spoke as the guys briefly stopped their regimens to wave as they proceeded towards the exit.

*Ch*apter 4

Summer and Floyd Gable feasted at the locally renowned Dan Fisher's upscale seafood restaurant. Floyd was the guy which Summer had been matched with through the internet dating portal.

After their date, she gave him a nice goodbye kiss. "Can I come in for a while?" he asked.

"No. Not tonight."

"I thought maybe we could get cozy."

"No Floyd!" Summer emphatically stated.

"I was hoping you would perhaps provide me with some sexual pleasure." He wouldn't take no for an answer."

"I think you should leave Floyd!"

He grabbed Summer by an arm and held it tight.

"You are hurting me!"

"That what's wrong with you pompous over achieving bitches!" Floyd snapped.

She squirmed trying to break free of his grip.

"You are nothing like you described yourself. You have no idea of how to treat a woman?"

Floyd then grabbed her by both arms. Face to face with Summer he yelled. "You are nothing! Do you hear me? You are nothing!" Summer was thrown to the ground; stumped, and then kicked by Floyd with his steel toed boots.

Floyd jumped into his car and then sped away.

A car stopped in front of Summer's house. "Lady, are you alright? I saw you being attacked."

"No," Summer murmured.

"Stay there. Ma'am. Don't try to get up. I'm calling for help."

When summoned the police and paramedics arrived promptly. Tony Gonzalez explained to one of the investigating officers how he'd witnessed a man assaulting Summer. Tony when asked provided a physical description of the suspect and his vehicle.

After providing preliminary medical care the paramedics transported Summer to a nearby hospital. She was treated for head trauma, bruised leg tendons, a couple of sore ribs, a severely sprained left ankle, and a swollen face.

Derrick was leaving the Gym the next afternoon when he noticed Camilla staring down. "Looks like you have a flat tire," Derrick said.

"I need to call my roadside service."

"Don't worry. I'll be more than willing to change your flat."

"You shouldn't bother," Camilla responded. "I wouldn't want to inconvenience you."

"I insist."

"Go ahead, knock yourself out," Camilla wittingly flirted. She used the remote on her car keys to pop open the truck.

He removed the spare tire. "By the way, my name is Derrick. And you are?"

"I'm Camilla. I spoke to you the other week when I was with my friend girls. You and some other guy were working out on the high tension bars as we were leaving."

"That guy was my brother." The well-toned calves of her legs caught Derrick's attention as he replaced the tire. He was done in no time flat. "I'm finished," he said.

"How much do I owe you?" She grinned.

"You don't owe me anything." He reached into his wallet and pulled out one of his business cards. "Let me give you my card. I'm a sole proprietor of an architectural firm."

"You are also a great minister." She paused. "I'm a local pre-school teacher; and a member of your Grace Missionary Baptist congregation. I don't foresee a need for an architect."

"Just take my card Camilla."

"Derrick. I don't know what to say. Thank you. I should be going." Camilla waved bye.

*Ch*apter 5

Summer's Assistant Manager and Magazine Editor Barbara Bolton visited Summer at Chandler Morgatte Medical Center. Stopping briefly at the onsite gift store, she purchased Summer a bouquet of roses.

Minister Thomas Richardson of Our Lord and Savior Baptist Church was seated at Summer's bedside as Barbara entered. He rose to his feet. "I'm Minister Thomas Richardson. Summer is one of my parishioners. How are you? I don't think we've ever met; at least not personally." He extended a hand in welcome.

"I'm fine. Thanks for asking. My name is Barbara Bolton. I work at Summer's auspicious bridal company."

"I wish the same could be said about Summer. Her parents Darnell and Deidra Reed stepped out to grab a bite. As you can see the pervert roughed up your girl pretty bad. She was in intensive care up until today. The attacker is still on the loose."

"I took Summer up on an invitation to visit your church about three weeks ago. I really enjoyed the service. Beverly Dawkins a friend from work accompanied me. We felt at home. Beverly and I are looking for a church home."

"Feel free to revisit anytime. We're about the business of the Lord. At Our Lord and Savior Baptist we welcome everyone with open arms."

"Thanks for the invitation. I'll be sure to revisit."

"Summer often brags about you being second in command at Summer's Bridal Fashions."

Summer opened her eyes. "Hi. Minister Richardson."

"Hi. Sister Summer."

"How are you?" Barbara asked.

"Not well," Summer said groggily. "How are things at the office?"

"Don't worry about the office. You should concentrate on getting well. I have everything under control." Barbara replied as Summer drifted back to sleep.

Summer's parents returned from lunch at the hospital café.

Barbara embraced and greeted them. "How are you two?

"We're fine," Darnell and Deidra responded in unison.

"How are you Barbara?" Deidra asked."

"I'm okay! Summer was awake!" Barbara exclaimed. "She spoke to us!"

"She is heavily medicated," Deidra pointed out. "She keeps going in and out of consciousness."

Darnell acknowledge Barbara. "Our daughter is blessed to have you as a friend and a trusted business associate."

"Let us pray." Everyone joined hands. Minister Richardson asked the Lord for a speedy recovery for the battered member of his flock.

Brenda dropped by the hospital the next morning during visiting hours.

Summer was more lively and coherent.

"My parents, Minister Richardson, and Barbara visited last evening."

"Looks like somebody tried to kill you." Brenda said.

"Thanks to Floyd Gable, I feel like hell warmed over. The bastard verbally abused and physically attacked me because I didn't invite him into my house for sex after our date. Floyd was the guy I mentioned meeting over the internet."

"Summer that is sick. How could anybody be so brutal?"

*Ch*apter 6

"How is my dear sister? Shouldn't you be at home still recuperating?" Bill spoke as he walked through Summer's open office doorway. Summer mounted her crutches. She hobbled in his direction before he could utter another word.

"It's been a month since I was brutally assaulted", Summer said. "I'm fine." She did a balancing act as the two embraced. "The doctor gave me the okay to return to work days ago. However, I waited until today. So what brings you to the city?"

"I flew in early this morning to personally scope out a proposed site for my law firm's new office in Lower Manhattan. More importantly, I'm here to check on my little sister. I wanted to visit you in the hospital; but a drawn out court case in Los Angeles prevented me from flying out any sooner. Mom and Dad kept me up to date on your condition. You were constantly in my prayers."

"Thanks," Summer said politely. "It's almost noon. Why don't we cut out of here and go somewhere for lunch. You do have time for lunch. I hope."

"The timing couldn't have been better. My meeting with my realtor is not for another two hours."

"There's a family restaurant nearby with raving reviews. Its name eludes me. However, I would love to give it a try."

On the way over to the restaurant Summer texted messaged Deidra. Surprisingly, she received an immediate response.

"Mom said Hi. She is happy that you are here." Summer returned a message that she is loved and to take care.

At the restaurant Bill offered his assistance. "Summer, I would love to personally prosecute your attacker."

"Detective Captain Mueller of the local police Department's investigations unit said they have posted in the news media a man wanted picture from the internet of my attacker."

"How did they to obtain their lead?"

"My friend Brenda Jamison alerted them to the internet website where I met Floyd. The authorities said he used fake credentials when he signed with the online dating service."

"So he was quite crafty. You are probably not his only victim."

"I will keep you informed as Captain Mueller's investigation progresses. Now. If I can get rid of these crutches, I'd be happy. I've been tempted on a number occasions to toss them."

"Sis. I believe the good doctor has your best interest at heart. Just hang in there."

"I'm scheduled to be reevaluated by the doctor on tomorrow."

*Ch*apter 7

A young lady spoke softly as Derrick answered his work phone. "Hi Derrick. I'm Camilla. I don't know if you recall me."

"I do. I was hoping you would call."

"A couple of weeks ago I didn't do such a great job of thanking you for your help at the Gym."

"Listen Camilla, I said don't worry. I would love to pick you up for dinner and a movie.

"For a minster, you don't waste time," she said.

"And neither do you. That's why I believe you called." Camilla provided him with her phone number and address.

"I'll pick you up about 7:30," Derrick added.

"Take care," she sighed lowly and then disconnected.

"He leaned back in his chair as a fleeting thought crossed his mind. *Hopefully she has the smarts to go along with her good looks and bubbly personality.*

Summer wringed her hands at her desk. Sasha Mills who had made an unplanned visit delivered heart-wrenching news. "The committee decided in order for you to compete you'll have to change your entry plan." Sasha's words cut like a dagger. "The rational was simple: Sid submitted the plan first, although you continue to contend it's yours."

Summer was speechless as she reflected on the time and funds expended in putting together what she perceived would be their winning entry. "Sasha! I'm devastated. I was severely beaten! I was sent to the hospital with life threatening injuries; only for you to deliver yet another crushing blow!"

"Calm down," Sasha called out to her long time business associate. "I am not in agreement with my colleagues' decision."

"I know," Summer quickly interjected. "I'm just venting."

"The committee would like for you to sign this formal agreement to change your competition plan or withdraw."

Summer resented the committee's finite ultimatum. "I won't allow myself to be coerced into making a rash decision. I am going to seek legal counsel."

Sasha eventually left without Summer's signature.

Derrick's assistant, Mable Bennett patched through a call. "A Ms. Summer Reed is on line two. She states the call is not of a personal but business nature."

"Thank you, Mable."

"Hi Derrick. If you have a moment, I have some good news."

"Sure Ms. Summer. What's on your mind? Let me guess. You finally realize what you'd be missing by not being my lady."

"Don't get your hopes high. And don't flatter yourself. I have a proposition for you; however, I am not included as a perk."

"I'm not quite sure what you mean."

"You stood out from the competition to design my new fashion boutique. I would like to offer you the job. But that would be contingent on us coming to terms."

"I have some preliminary drawings. We should have dinner so we can go over them. You will find them quite appealing."

"I should have a free spot on my schedule in a few nights." Summer checked her digital day planner to confirm the exact day and time.

"Great. We have a date. I'll email over the drawings in the meantime for you to mull over."

Summer provided Derrick with her email address and cell number.

A few hours later, Derrick was wining and dining Camilla at Akira D's a world class sushi restaurant.

Sitting awaiting their waitress, Camilla struck up a conversation. "I'm surprise a professional man of the clergy like you would still be available. You must have someone in your life." She awaited a response.

"You're right. I would have liked to have gotten to know a special lady."

"What happened?"

"I didn't pass her eligibility test. She doesn't date divorcees nor men which have been romantically involved with past or present friends."

"I'm quite the opposite. I am too a divorcee. So I would never hold that against you. If a relationship is truly over those that were involved should be free at will to forge new relationships."

"I agree."

On the heels of their dining experience Derrick treated Camilla to a Ted Denson premier action thriller movie debut.

*Ch*apter 8

Summer, Brenda, Barbara, and Jasmine visited B. J. Lawson's Bar and Grill for a ladies night out. Barbara planned the outing to get Summer's mind off her troubles.

After the afore-mentioned scheduled visit to her doctor, Summer no longer walked with the aid of crutches.

The regular Saturday night crowd was out in force.

Jasmine had been Summer's Personal Business Assistant until she was let go for being unreliable. Summer couldn't ever depend on Jasmine to show up for work; and when Jasmine did manage to show, she had alcohol on her breath."

Summer jumpstarted their talk. "Jasmine. I selected your ex male friend Derrick Hamilton to be my architect pending us finalizing our deal."

The bartender mixed their drinks.

Jasmine boasted. "Girl, I told you he's the best. You made the right choice. If you want to have a first class boutique, Derrick will make it happen."

"That's not all he interested in..." Barbara sarcastically interjected.

Summer butted in before she finished. "I agree. Derrick is obsessed by me." Summer stated. "Jasmine. I made it clear to him; I do not date my friends' ex mates."

Ladies let's not get testy." Brenda asked for cool heads to prevail. "Remember we are all friends."

Jasmine raised her eyebrows. "Who Derrick dates shouldn't be and isn't my concern," she declared nonchalantly. "We're no longer an item. He's yours for the taking." Jasmine gulped down a drink.

"I gave all applicants a fair chance to design my new boutique. And Derrick won out. Mr. Hamilton will just have to keep his personal feelings to himself."

Jasmine over indulged in alcohol as usual. Having had their fill of chatter eventually the girls said their goodbyes and departed.

Barbara dropped off Jasmine at her Brooklyn loft. She staggered upstairs into the decrepit awaiting dwelling.

Summer kicked off her flats to rest her feet as soon as she reached home. She took note of a text message on her iPhone from Bill. It simply stated: *Just to say hi.*

Still outraged over the fashion committee's decision, Summer phoned Bill to ask his legal opinion.

"I'm being treated unfairly. I've received a demand from the overseeing committee for the fashion show to either change my plan for the competition or gracefully bow out."

"I wouldn't think a committee would purposely cause harm to a participant without reason. Something prompted their action."

"A Mr. Sid Edelman entered a plan which mirrors mine."

"How did that happen?"

"When my ex Fashion Consultant Fay Edwards stopped working for me she went to work for Sid Edelman's Bridal Wear."

"That's quite a coincidence," Bill noted.

"Mentally and financially I would take a loss. It's just not right."

"I have a friend who owes me a favor," Bill disclosed. "He is the esteemed well known New

---

York City Civil Attorney Courtland Davidson. I will contact him on your behalf."

"Thanks Bill. I knew you'd come through. "

"Courtland will let you know if you have a case.

*Ch*apter 9

Summer and Derrick met at locally well-known Rolo's Gourmet Restaurant for their planned business dinner.

"You are here with me; but your mind is light years away." Derrick shared his observation.

"You are right. I am at my wits end. But that's not why I'm here. I was thoroughly impressed with your preliminary renderings. Either would fulfill my boutique design requirements."

The waiter interrupted them to serve their meal taken from Rolo's exclusive Specialty Country Foods and House Wines Menu.

Derrick assisted Summer in whittling the pickings to a final design for the new boutique.

"I'll have my attorney draw up an agreement." He closed his briefcase.

"Okay. I'll look forward to the final draft." Summer took a sip of red wine. She took a moment to savor the taste.

"I'm scheduled to attend an architectural conference and dinner at the locally owned five star R. L. Stevenson Resort Hotel. My invitation gives me the option to bring a guest. I would love for you to accompany me." Derrick provided the date and time.

"Why ask me? You should ask someone else."

"Stop pitying yourself," Derrick replied. "It's my understanding you were befriended. You wouldn't do anything dishonest.

"Are you sure Mr. Hamilton?" She responded with playful sarcasm. "Do you really know me that well?"

Derrick half smiled. "So what's your decision?"

Summer pretended not to hear the question. "Tonight's dinner is great. Thank you."

"And what is your decision?" Derrick again asked.

"I will have to get back with you. I have an out of town business engagement. I'll see if I can reschedule."

"My daughter Angel is a model."

"Really. I am not at all surprised."

"Angel started doing commercial photo shoots when she was just a toddler; and can be credited for having formalized training in dance and modeling. I mentioned your upcoming competition."

Oh. You just happened to bring it up..."

"Yes. I did."

"Angel would like to attend. I pray the Lord will work everything out. Your company deserves to be a part of the festive occasion."

"You and your daughter would love the show."

"The timing of the show couldn't have been better. Both of my kids will be on hand."

"I look forward to meeting your kids, especially your daughter.

*Ch*apter 10

Sunday at 11:00 a.m. Minster Derrick Hamilton touched hearts as he rendered a sermon about the Prodigal Son. The Holy Spirit was evident as it flowed throughout the vast edifice of Grace Missionary Baptist Church. Sisters caught up in the Word of the Lord shouted among the pews and in the isles.

Following the benediction parishioners slowly gravitated towards the exits.

"Summer Reed," Derrick lightly bellowed. "May I have a moment?"

Summer and Deidra stopped in their tracks. Deidra watched as a smile lit up her daughter's face.

Making his way through a crowd Derrick walked over. "Hi Summer, it's nice to see you. Let me guest. The young lady standing to your right is your mother."

"Yes. You are right as usual," Summer replied.

"I'm Deidra Reed."

"It's nice to meet you, Mrs. Reed. Summer undoubtedly inherited your beauty."

"Thanks. I'm honored to meet you Minister Hamilton or should I say Derrick."

"You can call me, Derrick."

"In addition to Derrick being the minister of this great church; he's also the architect I have chosen to design my new boutique.

"So you're a business man. Your debonair suave demeanor leads me to believe you're probably quite a ladies man too. Hopefully, you're not planning on breaking my daughter's heart."

"I would never dream of breaking your daughter's heart. I would love to get to know Summer better."

"And I would love to know him better."

Derrick chuckled. He felt Summer finally warming up to him.

"Summer mentioned you are from Atlanta."

"Yes. I am. I often visit my offspring in New York and California. Tomorrow, I'll be flying back to Atlanta."

"If it's the Lord's will Mrs. Reed, who knows, maybe we'll meet again."

"I hate to shorten our conversation. Mom still has to pack. We have plans for the afternoon. Maybe next time, you'll get to meet my father."

*Ch*apter 11

Fay was spotted as she whizzed through the reception area of Summer's Bridal Fashions.

"Stop! Excuse me! You need permission to go back there!" Beverly yelled.

Fay's week day off from work mission was to dispel a blatant lie.

As Fay crossed threshold of the door of Summer's office, Summer viciously disapproved. "Get out! You are no longer welcome here!"

Fay aggressively strutted over to confront her ex-boss as if she was about to attack. "You are going to hear me out Ms. Summer!" She shouted with hands on hips.

Jumping to a standing position, Summer slammed her desk with her hands. "I'm going to tell you one more time! Leave before I call security!"

Fay ignored the threat. "You don't know everything. Your assumption is wrong. I did not tell Sid about your plan."

"You are lying!" Summer let loose a verbal tirade. "You're trying to feed me a bunch of bull! And I don't want to hear it! Get the hell out!"

"If you would like to know who is responsible for the leak you should ask Jasmine, your friend, and ex personal assistant. She is having an affair with Sid. Jasmine probably has the answers to your questions. Now if you will excuse me, I'm through here." Fay turned to leave.

A security officer entered. "Are you alright Ms. Summer?"

"I'm fine. Kindly, escort Ms. Fay out. She should not be here."

"I could detain the intruder for trespassing; and call the cops."

"No. Just follow my instructions. Make sure she leaves."

Trailed closely by the officer, Fay left the premises. Concerned employees watched in awe.

"Hold all my calls," Summer instructed Beverly. "I'm taking the rest of the day off. I need to clear up a personal-business matter."

Summer's sports car tires squealed as she peeled out of the parking lot. She traveled to Brooklyn looking for Jasmine's address. Summer stumbled upon Jasmine sitting on a neighbor's stoop; hair tied up in a black scarf, wearing a low cut sundress, and sporting dark shades to conceal her bloodshot eyes.

"What the hell are you doing here?" Jasmine lashed out.

"Look at you, smashed as usual. Aren't you the least bit concerned about your alcohol addiction? Don't you see what it is doing to you?"

Jasmine body language displayed displeasure as she repeated her earlier question. "Cut the crap! Why are you here?"

"You know why I am here. You are having an affair with Sid Edelman."

"What business is that of yours?"

"You are the leak that told him of my plan for the competition. You of all people know how much I wanted to win."

"You are delusional. Why discredit you?"

"I fired you would be the first reason. Secondly you're mad that your ex male friend Derrick is interested in me."

"I am not holding a grudge or harboring any ill feelings towards you. And please let's not talk about Derrick again."

Jasmine witnessed Summer's face tightened. Summer threw both hands into the air. "Your psycho ass has strewed up my life!" She shouted. "Sid should at least apologize to me. He knows what you've done."

Jasmine's eyes flooded with tears. "I haven't done anything. Why don't you believe me?" She began to sob. "And if I were the snitch, Sid is not going to leave me. He loves me." She kept pouting.

"You are pitiful and crazy!" Summer thundered. "You are being used by a married man! Wake up and smell the coffee. If you were a worthy mistress, Sid wouldn't think twice about moving you out of this hell hole."

Jasmine jumped up from the stoop. "You don't know what in the hell you are talking about!

"Oh! I think I do."

"Oh! No you don't! For your information, I'm about to be evicted. Sid offered to help. I accepted. Thanks to Sid I'll be moving out into a nice condominium."

"You are a sad excuse for a friend," Summer hollered out. "You're a thorn in my butt after all I've done or tried to do for you."

"Get back into your car and leave before I put my foot..." Jasmine growled but decided not to finish her statement.

"We are done Jasmine!" Summer shouted back. "You confirmed what I wanted to know! You are trifling! And I don't ever want to see you again!"

*Ch*apter 12

In the Aquarius Manhattan Bowl lounge, Derrick and Brad shot a game of pool as they awaited the kick off of the Alley Cats Bowling League. Derrick's company, Hamilton Architectural Designs sponsored their team the Gospel Architects.

"And filling out the final spot on the team is Camilla," Brad imitated a sportscaster. "How did you manage to convince Camilla to join?"

"You do realize how ridiculous that sound." Derrick decided to play along. "It wasn't as difficult as you may think. Camilla and I were thinking of things we have in common. She mentioned bowling as a favorite past time in which she hadn't participated in a while. I asked if she'd like to join our team and she accepted."

The off character spoof ended. "You seem to resent your decision to have Camilla play."

"Brad. You are right, I am troubled. I shouldn't mislead Camilla. Summer is the one that tugs at my heart. She might not take kindly to someone I have been dating, namely Ms. Camilla, being on our team."

"I won't tell. If you don't."

"I wish it was that simple, I don't want to lose Summer. Camilla was an afterthought when I didn't get my way initially with Summer."

Derrick chalked his cue stick and then forced the 8 ball into a side pocket to win.

The brothers joined their team members at their assigned lanes to bowl to establish their individual handicaps. League play would officially start the proceeding Friday.

The next day, Derrick dropped in unannounced to Summer's place of business. He informed Beverly of his desire to surprise Summer.

"She just completed a meeting with an insurance executive. If you go now, you'll get to see Ms. Summer before her next scheduled appointment."

Derrick stepped through the doorway of Summer's office carrying a bouquet of freshly cut roses.

Summer was noticeably perturbed. She managed a tense smile. Derrick presented the flowers and then gently kissed her cheek.

"Thank you." Why are you here? Do you have our contract?"

"My attorney is still working on it."

"So. Why are you here?" Summer asked.

"You are not serious. My showing up with roses should be an indication. I am not here to do business. I am here for you."

"Stop dreaming. I'm not going to fall head over heels for you. It's not going to happen."

Derrick futilely tried to connect with Summer's inner soul. "I understand you're downhearted. Your moody behavior is most likely due to your current work fiasco."

"By the way, your ex-girlfriend Jasmine was the witch which derailed my effort to be this year's fashion competition winner. She's having an affair with Sid Edelman. I have since apologized to Fay Edwards my previous fashion merchandiser. I had accused Fay of being the culprit. You never met Fay. She is quite a character."

"How did Jasmine and Sid end up in a relationship? They are like night and day."

"Sid is like any married man. He likes a little something on the side; especially if the female looks at all halfway decent, and pays him half the attention he no longer gets from his wife."

"You never got back to me. The New York Architectural Ball is fast approaching, I still need to know if you will be accompanying me."

"I meant to get back to you. I won't be able to attend. I wasn't able to get out of my prior engagement. If you're still in need of a date, I suggest you find someone else."

Derrick's spirit was broken. "I don't understand. Should I find someone else as you suggest or leave the door open for you?" Summer gave Derrick the silent treatment. "I'll leave the door open. Let me know if things change."

Chapter 13

"Summer, pull up a chair, we need to talk."
Barbara was disheartened.

"Is everything alright?" Summer asked. "I hope you are not the bearer of more bad news."

"The readers are demanding answers. As your social media columnist and chief editor, I'm at a lost as to how I can best address their concerns. The majority gives you the benefit of the doubt and the rest would like you to come clean with an admission of guilt. Hopefully you will arm me with the right words to relay."

"Barbara. We can't please everybody. I will prepare a statement to assure my subscribers that I'm innocent of all alleged impropriety. Check your email later this afternoon for the explanation copy."

"The mushrooming effect of this scandal is exploding all over the internet with your image taking a serious hit."

"Most of the negatively publicity online probably can be addressed through our Facebook and Twitter accounts. I will go online with my own posts in an effort to squash the wrongful information being disseminated."

"If I am correct in my recollection, you were to meet with your attorney." Barbara altered the conversation.

"I wrapped up my consultation with him prior to coming in to speak with you."

"So how did it go?"

"It was pretty much a fact finding mission by Attorney Courtland Davidson. My brother Bill referred him."

Barbara tried to remain optimistic. "We should continue praying for a favorable outcome; while pressing ahead."

*Ch*apter 14

The night of the annual New York Architectural Ball, Summer decided to surprise Derrick. Against Summer's better judgment, she inquired at the front desk of the R. L. Stevenson Resort Hotel as to whether she would be able to join Derrick. Summer thought to herself; *I am going to hold him to his word. He said I still could join him if I should change my mind.*

"I'm a guest of Derrick Hamilton. I was delayed due to a prior engagement."

The maître d took a moment to check the guest roster. "Ms. Reed only one guest is allowed per invitation. I'm sorry if you were advised differently."

After leaving the hotel lobby walking back through the parking garage, she made another ill-timed decision.

Derrick answered his cell phone as it started to vibrate. "Hi this is Derrick Hamilton. Please hold." Failing to press the hold button, Derrick stopped speaking to address the waiter.

The waiter placed a well done steak dinner in front of Camilla. "You must be Mrs. Hamilton."

"No. I am Camilla Watson. We are not married."

"The steak is mine," Derrick said. I ordered it medium rare."

"I apologize. Give me a moment. I'll remove it from your tab and I'll return with your correct order." He then presented Camilla with her sautéed oyster dish.

Derrick resumed the call. "Thanks for holding. May I ask who is calling?"

"My meeting ended early. I'm back in town."

"Summer!" Derrick was caught off guard. "I can't talk right now." His eyes shifted toward Camilla. She looked as if a bad taste had suddenly entered her mouth.

"I'm confused." Summer sounded stressed. "I rushed back to town so I could join you. Our agreement was I could still attend your gala if by chance things changed."

"We'll talk about it later."

"Why can't we talk now?" She insisted.

Derrick did not respond.

"Who is Camilla? Summer demanded. "You mentioned her name as I was supposedly holding."

"Call me tomorrow. I'll explain everything."
Derrick hung up without warning.

"Who was that on the phone?" Camilla asked.
"No don't tell me. It was Summer. On your
untimely or should I say unexpected call you
blurted out Summer's name. Summer is the
woman you spoke about prior to our first date.
According to you, Ms. Summer turned you down
for tonight's gala. I'm a fool. You are still obsessed
by Summer, which is understandable. She is more
your equal."

"Don't be so hard on yourself. Summer's call
took me by surprise too."

"I know. You couldn't wait to disconnect. After
tonight, we are through. I don't want to have
anything else to do with you."

Derrick pulled a handkerchief from his jacket in
an attempt to wipe away moisture beneath her
eyelids.

"Stop it! She yelled. "Don't try to pamper me!"

Camilla frowned as she looked at others seated
around the table. "Stop eyeing us!" She lashed
out. "My misfortune shouldn't be your concern!"

Burning rubber leaving the hotel's parking
garage, Summer pulled in front of another vehicle

on the ground floor. Swerving to avoid a collision the terrified drivers applied their brakes as tires squealed and echoed.

Chapter 15

In the early morning fog, Summer spotted a stocky silhouette of a man across the street from her home. The mysterious guy's eyes stayed fixated on Summer as she backed her car out of her garage onto the roadway. Wildly accelerating, Summer peeled off down the street.

Brenda and Summer would have a discussion later at work regarding the suspicious character.

"Could he be a stalker?" Summer asked.

"Who are you referring to?"

"Floyd Gable. He is the guy who assaulted me."

"The jerk could be out to harm you again," Brenda quickly noted. "You should be careful."

"I have encountered this guy several times within the last three weeks," Summer continued. "He appears to be following me for some ungodly reason."

"You should report your new information to the authorities."

"I plan to do that this afternoon. I have a meeting with Detective Captain Adam Mueller of the local police department."

Barbara walked into the breakroom. "How are you-ladies?"

"We are fine," Brenda said.

"Sid is in the hot seat with his wife Carlotta for having an affair with our friend Jasmine," Barbara revealed. She poured a cup of coffee, adding sugar, and creamer. "Carlotta moved out into an extended stay hotel."

Barbara joined the ladies at their table.

"Are you serious?" Summer queried.

Barbara eyes rolled. "Honey girl. Carlotta walked out on him. She's threatening divorce. Apparently this wasn't the first time he cheated."

"How did she just happen to find out about the affair?"

"Summer it doesn't matter how…," Brenda sternly asserted. "Sid don't deserve compassion. Some men are just dogs!"

"The misfortune suits him," Summer stressed. "The man refuses to show any remorse for my current predicament. Granted he didn't wrong me intentionally. Jasmine led him blindly down that path."

"You're right," Barbara agreed. "Sid should confess. We shouldn't have to watch our competitors on stage; knowing we should also be on the program."

Summer met with Captain Mueller of the local police department. "I may have driven past the pervert this morning. As I was leaving for work I glimpsed a guy in the early morning fog standing across the street from my house. I think it may have been Floyd Gable. If he wasn't wearing a baseball cap, sporting a beard, and a goatee there wouldn't be any doubt."

"Captain Mueller stroked his chin. "You're not alone. During the last two months a half dozen other women have come forth with the same complaint of a stalker. All the victims appeared to have described the same guy. He seems to be infatuated by women in the fashion industry all with listings on social media and internet dating portals.

Captain Mueller showed Summer a deposit sketch.

"That's him." Summer glared at the crudely drawn rendering. "That's the stalker that has been following me for the last three weeks. Compare the sketch to the picture of Floyd and you'll see the striking resemblance."

"I made the comparison while you were on your way over. I derived at the same conclusion. I'm going to have a few of my undercover agents tail you. You may be able to breathe a little easier if by chance the guy turns out to be Floyd."

*Ch*apter 16

Summer visited Bill's Lower Manhattan east coast law office. It was move in day for the firm. She took note of the firm's attorneys and other essential personnel dutifully setting up their work spaces along a long sprawling hallway. A gold plate was attached to a door bearing the name Attorney William (Bill) Reed. She knocked. But no one answered. Summer walked back out to the reception area.

"Hi. You must be Emily Steel the voice which answered sometimes when I called my brother Attorney Bill Reed before your move from California."

"Yes. It's nice to meet you, Ms. Summer. Bill often brags about you. He calls you his workaholic sister. I relocated to New York City to be closer to my aging mother. I plan to check out some of the local law schools. I aspire to be a lawyer or maybe even a judge someday."

Emily noticed a sudden change in Summer's demeanor. A faint look appeared in her eyes.

"Are you okay?" Emily pulled a plastic cup from a dispenser attached to a nearby water fountain. "I'm going to get you some water."

Summer's knees buckled as she lost consciousness and then collapsed.

Emily called 911 as she took Summer's pulse.

"911. What's your emergency?"

"I would like to report that my boss' sister has fainted at my workstation. She fell awkwardly to the floor after bumping her head on a glass enclosed section of my work desk." Emily took a deep breath. "Her name is Summer Reed. Summer still has a pulse."

Emily was given instructions as how to assist until the paramedics arrived.

Bill heard a siren on his way back to work after lunch. A medical transport vehicle rapidly progressed towards his office after turning at the traffic light directly in from of him.

The light changed to green. Bill proceeded on his way. He neared the building witnessing paramedics frantically entering through the front entrance.

In the parking garage he hastily searched for a space and then parked. Rushing off the elevator exiting onto the floor of his office, Bill's worse fear was realized. Emergency medical specialists hoisted his sister onto a stretcher and then whisked her away.

Emily tapped Bill on the shoulder. He turned.

"I was talking with your sister; she collapsed. I called the paramedics. She's being transported to the local hospital for further evaluation and treatment."

Bill tore out of the building and then rushed over to the nearby medical center. He patiently awaited an update on Summer's condition.

Dr. Don Jeffers eventually briefed him. "Summer has a brain clot and has lapsed into a coma."

"Firstly, Summer fainted. Why? William asked."

The Doctor provided an inconclusive response. "The reason she fainted could've been from stress or a number of other reasons."

In the weeks that ensued, Bill took time off from work as much as possible to be by Summer's side.

Chapter 17

Derrick startled Beverly as she sorted the daily mail.

Wittingly Beverly commented on the bouquet of roses Derrick held. "Those must be for Summer. You're still trying to win Summer's affection."

"I made a costly error in judgment recently."

"You are here to plead for understanding and forgiveness."

"Yes. If Summer is not busy, I would like to surprise her with flowers. I'm hoping they'll loosen the tension between us."

"That will not be possible. Summer hasn't been at work for the last two days."

"She has been under a lot of stress lately. Taking time off from work to recuperate is not a bad idea."

"Summer's situation isn't that simple. She's at Chandler Morgatte Medical Center, once again, on life support."

Derrick slumped over Beverly's desktop. "I'm going to head over to the hospital. Give me a moment to regain my composure."

At Chandler Morgatte Medical Center, still noticeably shaken, Derrick waited his turn in line to check in with the front desk receptionist.

"I am here to see Summer Reed."

"Summer is in the intensive care unit. Only members of her immediate family are allowed to visit."

Derrick stood silent. A voice behind him spoke on his behalf.

"Summer Reed is my daughter. Derrick is my son. Go ahead Derrick, sign in."

Derrick thanked Deidra on their way to the ICU. "The Lord sent you in the nick of time. Do you really think of me as a son?"

"It shouldn't matter what I think; you cared enough to be at my daughter's bedside with a bouquet of roses."

Derrick and Deidra approached the nurse station down the hall from Summer's room.

"I'll take the flowers," Nurse Emma Reaves said. "ICU patients cannot have them."

Derrick veered at Summer's mother. "I would like for you to have the flowers."

"She can pick them up on her way out."

Nurse Reaves supplied them with standardized sterilized garments, masks and gloves which they promptly donned after sanitizing their hands.

Tears welled up in the corners of Deidra's eyes as she watched her daughter lying comatose.

Deidra and Derrick talked among themselves and to Summer who though verbally unable able to communicate, occasionally changed her facial expression, and flexed her fingers."

"Where is Mr. Reed?"

"Darnell is flying in from Detroit. He was the keynote springtime graduation speaker at his Alma Mater, Carver Dixon University. The ceremony wrapped up about two hours ago."

"He'll be arriving later tonight. Am I right?"

"Yes." She looked Derrick square in the eyes. "I'm still elated that you cared enough to be here."

"Summer, I hope you were listening. Your mother likes me." A crease formed in Summer's face, which Derrick interpreted as a smile resulting from his off the cuff humor.

Deidra and Derrick took turns praying for a speedy recovery for Summer.

Derrick stayed at Summer's bedside until nightfall. "Take care, Mrs. Reed. It's time for me to head out."

He gently stroked Summer's right hand and then gave Deidra a friendly hug.

"Jot down my cell phone number. I'll keep you informed of Summer's condition."

"Thanks, Mrs. Reed."

*Ch*apter 18

Barbara listened to Summer's voicemail. All messages were as usual except one from Sid Edelman.

She returned the call. "May I speak with Mr. Edelman? I'm Barbara Bolton calling on behalf of Summer Reed."

"Mr. Edelman is on another call. Would you like to hold?"

"Sure. I'll hold." Multitasking, Barbara reviewed, and responded to emails."

"Sid speaking, how may I help you?"

"Hi Sid, I'm Barbara Bolton. I am Summer Reed's Assistant."

"Hi Barbara, I was hoping to speak with Summer. Is she not available?"

"No. She is not available. How may I help?"

"Darling, kindly put Summer on the phone!" Sid roared. "We have something important to discuss."

"That's not possible?"

"What isn't possible?" He elevated his voice.

"Summer is in the Intensive Care Unit at Chandler Morgatte Medical Center hooked to a respirator in a coma fighting for her life.

"Oh my God?" Sid cried out. "What have I done? My intent wasn't to harm Summer. Jasmine lied to me. Knowing the fashion Industry, I should have known the plan outlined was not Jasmine's. I was calling to ask Summer's forgiveness."

"Summer had already derived at that conclusion although Jasmine continues to deny being the turncoat."

"She not only destroyed my marriage by forging an adulterous relationship, she also caused me to screw up Summer's life. I have a meeting this week with the competition committee. I'm going to plead for their understanding to somehow allow us both to compete. Summer most likely would have approved of this gesture, don't you think?"

"I agree. She also would be overcome by your sudden show of compassion."

"She has to pull through. I have to let Summer know my true feelings," Sid stated. "I will get back to you once I meet with the committee."

*Ch*apter 19

Disgruntled Derrick watched as his team mates rolled their final practice balls. "We may have to forfeit tonight's games. I should have called our substitute bowler. I don't think Camilla is going to show."

"I think you are right," Brad replied.

"Where is your friend?" Team Captain Stan Thomas yelled to Derrick. "If Camila's cute little butt doesn't get here we're going to be disqualified from tonight's competition!"

Just as Stan finished his outburst, Camilla rushed through a nearby side entrance. "I never told anyone, I was punctual," she ranted unapologetically. "I'm here. Let's bowl."

"Try being on time going forth!" Stan scolded Camilla. "We all committed to be on time!"

"Yes. I know. We agreed to arrive at least fifteen minutes before start of play."

At the conclusion of game one Derrick visited the concession stand. He observed Camilla as she walked over to place an order too.

"I owe you an apology for my rude behavior." Camilla spoke softly.

"No apology should be given. Our classy night out caused a rift between Summer and I."

"How is Summer?" She asked."

"Summer fell and hit her head while attempting to visit her brother at his new law office. She's hospitalized clinging to life in a coma."

"Oh no!" Camilla exclaimed. I am deeply saddened."

Derrick and Camilla finished their purchases. Walking back to their lanes, Camilla spoke aloud an earlier thought. "I should have never gotten involved with you, Derrick Hamilton."

The night wore on and Camilla rolled a game winning tenth frame ball. It culminated in them winning all three league opening games against their first matched opponent Samuel's Hardware.

In leaving the alley, Derrick maneuvered his vehicle out of a cramped parking space. Derrick struck up a conversation on his way to dropping Brad back off to his house. "Baby brother. You may find this hard to believe. I was really hoping Camilla would not have shown. I feel like I am cheating on Summer. She remains in a coma; and I am bowling with Camilla, someone I know she despises."

"You should tell Camilla how you feel about Summer."

"I reemphasized that information tonight."

"And what happened?"

"I got the impression that she might quit the team."

*Ch*apter 20

Sid faithfully returned Barbara's phone call. "Hopefully the Lord will give credence to a heathen's plea. I have been praying for your boss' recovery."

"I'm sure the Lord will. So how did the meeting go with the competition committee?"

"I informed those in charge of Summer's medical condition. I let it be known their allegation lodged against Summer couldn't have be any further from the truth."

"I take that to mean you explained Jasmine's roll in the whole mess."

"Yes. I explained everything. The meeting concluded with them saying they'd forward the information to their attorney."

After briefly stopping to check in with the reservations clerk at Captain Sam's Seafood Restaurant, Derrick was escorted to a table where the Reed's awaited.

"Sorry I am late. But the traffic on the way over was unusually heavy."

"You must be the gentleman that Deidra spoke of so eloquently."

"And you must be Summer's father Mr. Darnell Reed." He stood back to his feet momentarily to shake their hands.

A smiling waitress appeared tableside with appetizers for the Reeds. "Your dinner will be served shortly."

She turned to Derrick. "I'm Tori your waitress. It's nice to meet you sir. May I take your order?"

"Yes Tori," Derrick stated. He ordered from the daily fresh catch menu."

"Would you like an appetizer? Coffee would be on the house."

"No thank you."

"Enjoy," Tori said.

Deidra took a sip of coffee. She frowned. "You probably would like to know how Summer is faring." She added more sugar.

"Yes. I can't get her off my mind."

"Her condition is stable. She's now breathing on her own."

Derrick thought to himself. *Summer's last memory of me was not at all good. Why am I here?*

"Are you okay?" Darnell asked. "You appeared to be in deep thought."

"I was thinking about the last conversation I had with your daughter. I'm fine."

"Summer has got to pull through. She has to witness her new boutique that you are designing."

"Thanks Mrs. Deidra. I'm going to make Summer, you, and your husband proud."

"It's nice to see young black men succeed," Deidra commented.

"Operating a top notch architectural firm in these tough economic times can't be easy." Darnell added.

"You're right. Times have been hard."

"Darnell, Deidra and Derrick continued non-stop sharing common topics of interest."

Tori interrupted them temporarily to serve their meal. The trio acknowledged Tori for her astuteness.

"Why did you decide to become an architect?" Deidra queried.

"My father was an architect. In fact he founded Hamilton Architectural Designs over forty five years ago. He inspired me. I'm caring on his legacy."

"That's really touching," Darnell said.

"I obtained my architectural Bachelor of Science degree from my parent's college alma mater Atlanta Stevenson University. My father and mother were born in France. By fate they met at ASU. I was blessed to be raised in a home with two loving parents."

"According to Summer your father died while on a fishing expedition."

"About seven years ago on a fishing trip 50 miles off the coast of Florida he suffered a major heart attack. A medical rescue transport helicopter was dispatched. It reached the vessel too late. Dad already had taken his last breath. Mom died a year later from old age. She was found dead in bed fully clothed."

Deidra and Darnell expressed sorrow to Derrick for the lost off his parents. Conversation dwindled as they finished dinner.

Leaving the restaurant, Derrick paid the total tab for the evening.

"Thanks for joining us. We enjoyed your conversation. You made our evening special."

"The pleasure was all mine," Derrick replied.

"We would love to return the favor," Darnell offered. "If you are ever in Atlanta give us a holler."

*Ch*apter 21

Barbara halted Brenda in the hallway on the way to their work area to share in an early morning office chat.

"Detective Captain Mueller stopped by yesterday. I provided him with an update on Summer," Barbara said. "As you know, Summer's condition has improved."

"I know. So how is the detective's investigation going?" Brenda asked.

"I'm shocked and torn by something he revealed. According to him the psycho jerk has now raped and assaulted a woman."

"How could he…" Brenda stopped in midsentence seemly stunned.

"Her name is Lori Benson," Barbara disclosed. "She is a local model."

"The name sounds familiar."

"Lorie performed freelance work for us on several occasions. She has been studying abroad. On college break, she flew in last week to visit her parents.

"Oh, I remember Lorie," Brenda said. "She was the young lady Summer and I had surmised was on the verge of being anorexic. How is she faring."

"Lorie's condition is stable at one of our local area hospitals," Barbara replied.

"He committed rape." Brenda shook her head. "That's really scary. I hope the twisted jerk doesn't kill anybody. We'll talk more on break."

Barbara still distraught continued to her office. She returned a call from the competition committee.

"Hi Sasha, I got your voice mail."

"Great. I have good news." But first, I should ask, how is Summer?"

"She is still in a coma but showing signs of maybe pulling through."

"I'll be sure to keep her in my prayers."

"So Sasha what's the good news."

"We have decided to allow Summer's Bridal Fashions to compete."

"You are kidding!"

"No. I am serious. We sent out a formal letter via mail today with stipulations to be followed."

"If only Summer was here to get the news everything would be perfect," Barbara responded.

Barbara went straight to Summer's house after work. She rang the doorbell. Deidra answered. "Come in. How are you? And how is the office?"

"I'm fine. And the office is fine. I have the news Summer had been waiting for before her unfortunate setback. The fashion committee has decided to allow Summer's Bridal Fashions and Sid Edelman's Bridal Wear both to compete."

Deidra tried to find the right word. "I'm happy! I'm overjoyed!" A wide smile lit up her face." I can't wait to whisper the news into Summer's ear. Hopefully it will lift her spirits. Have a seat. I have coffee percolating. Would you like a cup?"

"I'll have it black with a little sugar."

"I can throw in a tinge of honey for extra flavor."

"Okay." Deidra let out a sigh of relief. She smiled. "If you need me, let me know. I would love to help out at the office. I won't get in the way. As Summer's mother, I feel obligated to lend a hand."

"Thanks for the kind gesture. As I mentioned earlier; Mrs. Deidra, everything's fine at the office. You should keep your focus on Summer."

*Ch*apter 22

Raising the team's anxiety and anger, Camilla strolled into the bowling alley again late.

"Hi Derrick." Camilla's voiced sweetly resonated.

Lifting his eyebrows displaying a look of unbelief, Derrick struck up a conversation with the team's captain. "Camilla still needs to work on promptness."

"She'll be alright eventually," Stan replied. Your girl is shaping up to be our best bowler."

Derrick and Camilla barely spoke as the night progressed. The Gospel Architects remained undefeated.

Awaiting a call from his kids, Derrick dozed off watching a sports legends television special.

A quarter of midnight, Derrick's cell phone awakened him. Roderick informed his father their plane would be landing in about forty five minutes at JFK Airport.

"Let your sister know that I'll be waiting when the plane touches down."

"Okay. See you then. Drive safely."

On the way to the Airport the unthinkable happened. Traffic slowed to a crawl. A massive auto accident delayed his plan to timely pick up Roderick and Angel. He tried calling his kids but their cell phones had been silenced. Arriving at the airport they began to worry after picking up their luggage from baggage claims.

Angel switched on her cell phone. "Where is Dad? He said he would be waiting."

Derrick had left a message on their cell phones explaining that he would be late due to an auto accident.

Angel promptly dialed her father. "Are you okay? You mentioned an auto accident."

"I'm fine; just a little shaken. Traffic is at a standstill. I watched emergency workers use a Jaws of Life device to pry open a mangled vehicle to remove a young girl. She appeared to be about your age." Derrick reflected on how precious his family and friends are in his life. He thanked God for his kids. "Traffic should start moving again soon. The tow trucks have arrived."

After finally picking up his precious Roderick and Angel, Derrick stopped at an all-night café.

His kids were hungry. It was a few hours before sunrise. He treated them to an early breakfast.

"Mom sends her love," Roderick said.

"I know. My children are the evidence of her love. My young lady will be going off to college soon to pursue her fashion merchandising dream."

"That remains my intent. And I'm still looking forward to meeting your friend Summer the fashion guru."

"Summer is more of a fashion mogul than a guru. She is extremely knowledgeable and highly respected in the industry."

*Ch*apter 23

Sunday Morning at Grace Missionary Baptist
Church, Deidra put forth a personal plea.
"Minister Hamilton, I would like to thank you, your
clergy, your staff, and magnificent parishioners for
keeping my daughter Summer humbly in your
prayers. Words cannot express my gratitude. I ask
for your continued prayers." Deidra glanced at
Derrick. "Minister Hamilton a few weeks ago lifted
Summer before you. Since then Summer has
shown signs of pulling through her coma. The
Lord listens to the fervent prayer of the righteous."

"Amen, hallelujah! Hallelujah!" Deaconate Dora
Smiley gestured towards heaven. "Ask and you
shall receive!"

As Deidra walked back to her pew, Derrick
followed with his own choice words. "Summer
holds a special place in my heart. She's a
remarkable woman and a dear friend." Bristling
chatter sprang forth. Derrick recaptured their
attention as he proceeded with the order of
service.

After the benediction Derrick and Deidra had a heart to heart talk. She provided him an update on Summer's condition.

"The Lord is good."

"Yes he is, Mrs. Reed. He is good, all the time."

"Let me tell you how good. Something interesting happened on yesterday. After having lunch in the hospital cafeteria, I returned to Summer's bedside, and her eyes were open. She said Hi Mom, mumbled something, and then drifted back into a deep sleep."

"That's encouraging."

"She may be coming around. I think the message may have been for you."

"On your next visit I would like you to deliver Summer a message."

"And what might that be Minister Hamilton?"

"You don't have to address me formally."

"Okay, Derrick. What should I tell my daughter? I know she cares for you. But I also know you broke Summer's heart. That disturbs me. However, we will talk about that later."

"Tell Summer that I love her dearly and that I think of her constantly."

"Those are really strong words from a man of God. Do you mean them?"

"Yes, Mrs. Reed."

"Hopefully, she will be touched by your new found sensitivity."

"My daughter Angel appears to be headed in our direction."

"If I might say, she is quite a looker. According to Summer, Ms. Angel aspires to be a highly sought after fashion model. That won't happen without hard work."

"My daughter and I both share the same work ethic. To be great: one should thrive for greatness."

Angel waved to Dennis Stallworth a new male acquaintance who was exiting the sanctuary. She approached Derrick and Deidra.

"Angel, I would like to formally introduce you to Mrs. Deidra Reed. She is Summer's mother."

"Hi, darling." Deidra embraced Angel. "How are you?"

"I am fine. And how are you, Mrs. Reed."

"I'm good. As a result of Summer's illness I look forward to introducing you to Summer's Bridal

Fashions and to the company's talented staff. I would love to give you the grand tour which Summer promised."

"Thank you. I had been waiting anxiously to meet with your daughter. I'll keep my fingers crossed; who knows, she might pull through while I am visiting."

"You're right. Who knows? She just might pull through. We'll give her a little time."

"We won't accept anything short of a miracle," Derrick added. The Lord raised Lazarus from the dead. He certainly can awake Summer from a coma."

"Dad can be so melodramatic at times."

"They all laughed."

"You should meet my son, Roderick. You'd probably take a liking to him too."

"Perhaps we will meet."

"Roderick couldn't wait to reunite with an old buddy. Otherwise he may have graced your presence today."

"Derrick. If Roderick is anything like my son was as a teen, I can understand. Teens often have their own agenda."

Chapter 24

Deidra's voice screamed over Derrick's cell phone speaker. "Summer has been released from the hospital! My daughter is finally home recuperating!"

"Great!" Derrick exclaimed. "When can I come over?"

"The doctor wants Summer to wait a couple more days before she interacts with anyone else. She's your same old Summer."

"Thank you Lord. Thank you. The Lord has answered our prayers."

Two days crept by and Derrick like clockwork showed up on Summer's doorstep.

For heaven sake!" Deidra yelled. "I'm coming!" Derrick kept on ringing the doorbell, and banging on the door, until finally she snatched it open.

"Hi Mrs. Reed."

"Hi sweetheart. Summer has been non-stop asking about you. Right this way." Deidra beckoned.

Summer was lying in bed watching television as Derrick made his entrance. Straightaway, she moved from a prone to an upright position.

Derrick grazed Summer's right cheek with a kiss.

"You gave me quite a scare," Derrick said. "Don't ever do that again." They laughed.

"When you visited me at the hospital, I knew you were by my side."

"And God has given us another chance," Derrick ecstatically replied.

Derrick and Summer's chat was brief. Summer laid back down; smiling, she drifted off to sleep.

On his way out Derrick asked Deidra's attention.

"Give me a moment. Deidra removed a platter of salt and pepper seasoned turkey wings from the oven. She brushed on a special barbecue sauce and then positioned them back onto the oven's top rack to finish baking.

"Mr. Hamilton, you have my undivided attention. How may I help you?"

"I wish your husband was here, so I could ask him too."

"You can start with me." She tightened the apron around her waist.

"I'm really fond of your daughter."

"I know," Deidra agreed.

"I would love for Summer and I to spend the rest of our lives together. But I would only ask for Summer's hand in marriage if her parents saw fit to bless our bond."

"Say no more. I would love to have you as a son in law. Now as far as Darnell's response; I'm sure he'll approve as well. I must say, however, this is sudden. You two have only known each other a short time."

"I want us to commit to each other. Our engagement wouldn't mean we're in a rush to marry."

The doorbell rang. "I wasn't expecting anyone." Deidra toweled off her hands. She walked from the kitchen into the grand room. Opening the door she stared into her husband's eyes. Deidra and Darnell spontaneously hugged and then kissed.

"You're home early. I wasn't expecting you until tomorrow."

"My plan changed. The airline allowed me to opt for an earlier flight."

"Honey we have a guest." She stepped aside. Darnell made his way inside.

"Hi Derrick. I see you got the same memo. I hopped on the first flight I could get out of Atlanta. My daughter is home. You're joining us for dinner. Am I Right?"

"I was going to ask him to stay for dinner but before I could get the words out of my mouth; you rang the doorbell."

"Your timing couldn't have been better. I gladly accept your offer."

If you two gentlemen will excuse me, I have food demanding my attention. Dinner should be ready soon.

Summer exited her bedroom. "Can't a girl get some rest? I deserve better. What's all this noisy chatter?" Summer strolled down the hallway right into her father's outstretched arms."

"Hi Summer. I got here as soon as I could. How are you?"

"I'm fine dad. My favorite two guys have made my day."

"Derrick agreed to have dinner with us."

"Summer, I accepted the invitation. I knew your father wouldn't take no for an answer. Your mom should be calling us soon."

"I'll see if she needs help setting the table. Excuse me." Summer joined Deidra in the kitchen.

"Mr. Reed. I hope you are ready for what I'm about to ask."

"I served two tours of war duty in Vietnam. I'm ready for anything."

"If your daughter will have me; I feel we should spend the rest of lives together. Your wife said earlier she wouldn't stand in our way."

"You would have my blessing as long as the Lord see fit for the union of marriage."

Everyone filed into the dining room. Darnell sat at the head of the table in keeping with tradition.

Summer shifted her head downward and then upward. "Derrick. I don't know what to think; I fell asleep, I awoke, and you are still here."

"Instead of leaving your mom and I talked about my commitment to her daughter. Your father and I have since had the same talk."

"I hope you're not going to put me on the spot tonight with a proposal."

"No. I'm just looking towards the future. Knowing your parents feelings in advance cannot hurt."

"Having to function as the first lady of a renowned mega church and as Mrs. Derrick Hamilton would be quite a challenge."

Derrick feeling led by the Holy Spirit refrained from further commenting.

*Ch*apter 25

Camilla hooked a ball flush into the strike pocket. The strike sealed the winning of the first of three games for the evening. Excitedly, Camilla high fived Derrick as they made eye contact with Summer who'd just entered the establishment.

A few minutes later, Camilla and her new found friend Briana waved as they were about to walk past Derrick chatting with Summer.

"I'll meet you back at the lanes." Camilla lifted her voice and spoke directly to Derrick ignoring Summer. "Two more wins and we'll be done for tonight. Briana and I are going to grab a couple drinks from the lounge. We have two more games to win," she reemphasized.

"Okay Camilla," Derrick responded. "See you back at the lanes."

Summer's anger exploded with his mentioning of the name Camilla. "You enjoy making my life pure hell! Pure Hell!" She stepped towards Camilla. "Otherwise you'd leave Derrick alone!"

Camilla stood speechless.

"Camilla. I'll meet you in the lounge." Briana excused herself from the sudden unpleasant drama.

"Camilla meet Summer Reed. I'm sorry for her outburst." Derrick paused and then spoke out again. "Summer! You are wrong! Camilla joined my team prior to you finally committing to our relationship. I think you owe Camilla an apology."

"I won't apologize!" Summer's facial muscles tightened." You two were an item! And you're still involved!

Camilla broke her silence. "You were recently critically ill. Am I right? And you're still recuperating. You should get a grip on your emotions."

Still livid Camilla darted back to the teams assigned lanes area.

The team captain watched Camilla as she bagged up her ball and then shoes. Both fist clinched, she let out a deafening scream.

"What's wrong?" Stan said.

"I think you should ask your team's sponsor Derrick Hamilton. At the crux of the matter is Derrick and his lady friend Summer."

"Perhaps you should rethink your action. If you leave we will forfeit our remaining two games."

"I have nothing more to say." Camilla gripped her gear and stormed out.

Derrick and Summer took their disagreement to the parking lot.

"How could you?" Summer further voiced her displeasure. "I thought we'd taken our relationship to another level."

"Just say the words and I will quit the team."

Summer softened her tone. "That would be awkward, since you are the sponsor of the team." She shook her head. "I gave Angel a tour of my business today. She kept bragging to my staff about her perfect father. Angel also mentioned you would be bowling tonight. That's the reason I'm here. And when I saw Camilla my heart sank."

"You vehemently dislike Camilla. I didn't want her to come between us. That's why I didn't mention her being on my team."

Summer's eyes cut like a knife. "You have a decision to make. You will either choose me or Camilla."

Summer arrived home. Bill was shooting the breeze with their parents.

"Bill I didn't expect to see you tonight."

Bill verbalized his observation. "You seem perturbed or should I say irritated."

"I dropped by the local bowling alley after work. It was quite an eye opening experience."

"What happened?" Bill asked.

"You were going to surprise Derrick," Deidra noted.

"Yeah. But I got a surprise instead. Guess who was with him. Camilla Watson! She bowls on his team. She was all up in his face. Yet Derrick claims I have nothing worry about."

"You probably expect me to take your side. Nevertheless, I'm going to give Derrick the benefit of the doubt. After all he is a minister."

"I hope you're right. Dad, I would like to know your perspective. How do you perceive this matter?

"I'm going to agree with you mother. Relationships should be built on trust. We should put this conversation to rest."

"I agree dad," Bill stated. "Summer, I have something to tell you. Sylvia won't be available for the fashion extravaganza. I know you were expecting to have your whole family in attendance. Unfortunately, Sylvia will be hosting a three day women's empowerment conference set in the San Francisco Bay Area the same week of the fashion gala."

"Although Sylvia won't be there, she'll still be sending your beloved twins Jay and Jaylene. Am I right?

"No, I'm sorry to say. They decided to forgo on the event too.

Another week went by and The Gospel Architects anxiously awaited Camilla again.

Derrick received a phone call. "Promise me, you won't get angry," Camilla pleaded.

"I'm already angry! Your team is waiting on you!

"I have a flat tire. I contacted my roadside service over an hour ago. I'm still waiting on their auto repair person who according to their 'Deluxe Guarantee' should have been here twenty minutes ago."

"Derrick scolded Camilla. "You should invest in some new tires! For Heaven's sake woman! You should think about your safety!"

"Apologize to the team for me. I'm sorry we're going to have to forfeit tonight's games."

Derrick assured her everything would be fine. "Don't worry. I followed the advice of the Lord.

"And God fixed it. Right?" Camilla added.

"Yes. He did. My son Roderick is our new relief-substitute bowler. He's going to fill in for you."

"I only joined the team to be near you. You led me to believe you cared."

"Okay. Camilla let's not go back down that road."

"I'm not a bad person. Why can't I find favor in the Lord? Even the Lord wants me out of your life. I'm quitting the team! We're done!" Camilla pressed the end of call button.

Derrick and his Gospel Architects with Roderick onboard would eventually go on to become the Alley Cats Bowling League Champions.

Chapter 26

A special momentous Sunday in June came to past.

"Grace Missionary Baptist clergy, members, and friends, I'd like to have your attention." Derick came down out of the pulpit. He reached out to Summer who was seated with her parents. "Summer Reed, will you accompany to the pulpit." She stood. Derrick and Summer locked hands as they proceeded up a single flight of stairs into the pulpit.

Derrick knelt and she turned to face him.

"Summer. I'm eternally grateful you're in my life. Each morning I awake thinking of you; and I pray we will always be together."

Summer smiled as she wiped a few tears from Derrick's face as she pledged her unwavering love. "I am yours today. And I'll be yours as we go forth. Derrick. We are together because God has sealed our fate."

Derrick unclenched his left hand revealing a diamond ring.

A complete silence came over the sanctuary. Derrick and Summer looked deeply into each other's eyes.

"Go ahead pastor! Ask your lady!" An elderly gentleman on a back pew shouted.

Derrick chuckled. She smiled. "Summer Reed. Will you marry me?"

"Yes Minister Hamilton-Derrick. I will marry you."

He glided the brightly shimmering engagement ring onto Summer's awaiting trembling finger.

Derrick stood to his feet; on impulse they embraced, and then kissed.

After delivering a heart-warming sermon, Derrick opened up the doors to the church.

The choir sang a song of invitation.

Summer was the first to join the minister at the altar.

Derrick held her close. "Would you like to address the congregation?"

Summer was caught off guard. She eyed Derrick and then the congregation searching for the right words to say. "Since I relocated to New York City several years ago, I have attended Our Lord and Savior Baptist Church. Thomas Richardson resides as the senior minister. I would love to move my membership by way of letter to Grace Missionary Baptist."

Summer along with the others which gave their life to the Lord for the first time were ushered to a nearby conference room to be further briefed and welcomed.

Sister Ida Pratt sought Summer's assistance in working with their women and youth ministries.

"Minister Hamilton thinks you would be a perfect fit for our youth department. I wholeheartedly agree. Without a doubt, you'd be an ideal role model for the youth especially the young ladies. Your excellent academic and professional credentials speaks for themselves."

"I'd be delighted to work with the youth ministry. The mentoring of young ladies, it's something I'm already accustomed; whether in person when given the opportunity, or through my quarterly fashion magazine."

"You're without a doubt God sent. You should also join our women ministry."

"Sure. I'd be delighted to hang with the ladies in whatever way or capacity the Lord should see fit."

"Welcome to Grace Missionary Baptist Church."

Summer looked for her parents but they wasn't to be found.

Derrick startled Summer as he walked up from behind. "I told your parents I would see you home."

"So they left without me."

"I'm afraid so... We have an engagement to celebrate."

"I agree. We should start by having lunch."

"Later we should have dinner. And afterwards we should catch an off Broadway musical in the midtown district."

"You remembered! I had been dropping subtle hints."

"I know. I already have the tickets."

All and all their engagement celebration went well. By end of the night they had made a pivotal decision not rush their marriage. Derrick surmised and Summer agreed that their engagement could last anywhere from six months to two years.

*Ch*apter 27

Spotlights crisscrossed the stage and runway as music blasted throughout the dark vastness of the Grand Royal Hotel Convention and Civic Auditorium. Lurking unbeknownst to Summer and others at the festive New York Bridal Fashion Show an unwelcomed guest lay in waiting. Magically the evening host appeared as the house lights were brought to full brightness.

The bridal competition as in years past showcased the latest in formal wedding attire.

Sid Edelman's Bridal Wear models were first to rock the runway wooing the crowd with each outfit shown. One would have thought that Sid and his guys and gals would have been the clear winner until his only real threat took stage.

Summer's selection of first class models with ties to various countries gave their entry a fresh international flavor. Summer's Bridal Fashions well-rehearsed troop took control of the runway as they mesmerized everyone in attendance. The fine garments were designed and assembled with the assistance of Summer's newly acquired in house materials buyer/consultant Glenis Webster and fashion designer Dennis Stoddard.

Angel's topnotch presentation floored Derrick. His daughter matched Summer's other girls performances with each twist and turn.

Derrick's only disappointment for the evening was that his son was not in attendance. Roderick was home bedridden with flulike symptoms.

The judges tallied and finalized all twenty five entrants' results. For the first time in the competition's brief history, Summer's Bridal Fashions was chosen the winner. Summer addressed the audience; firstly she gave thanks to God followed by a special shout out to her family. Winners of Summer's fashion magazine educational contest were also called upon to stand.

At the conclusion of the much heralded well-received production the troops paraded back onto the stage. Among those applauding in the balcony a guy stood with a black handkerchief over his hands. Shots rang out as the gunman was tackled by undercover cops. A bullet grazed Beth Ann one of Sid's models. Another stray bullet knocked out the lighting above a side exit. Crowds rushed through the remaining lit exits.

Derrick, Bill and Summer's parents made a beeline to the backstage side entrance. Summer was summoned and promptly came out to assure them she and Angel were fine.

Summer somewhat still panic-stricken shared what she witnessed. "I stared the shooter directly in the eyes for a split second before the ordeal unfolded. It was him! It was Floyd Gable the guy which assaulted me! He was apprehended by undercover cops!"

"Thank God they arrested the bastard," Deidra still unsettled responded.

"Yes," Darnell said. "We have been blessed. Our daughter can finally rest assured he's off the streets."

"I wished they could have made the arrest without incident," Summer added. "One of Sid's models Beth Ann was hit as we all scrambled to run off stage. I'm told she's okay. The bullet scrapped her right arm."

Derrick embraced Summer. "Floyd gave us all quite a scare. I'm happy you're fine."

"I'll do my best to make sure the jerk is penalized to the fullest extent of the law," Bill stressed.

Summer brought the brief conversation to a close. "If you all will excuse me, I have backstage tasks to finish."

The group waved to Summer as she turned away. They proceeded back out to the front stage area to the aftermath of the shooting.

Paramedics burst through the main entrance. Beth Ann was still lying on the runway. The medical professionals removed a makeshift tourniquet around her upper right arm. A guy which claimed to be a doctor had dutifully applied it to suppress bleeding. The superficial gunshot wound was non- life-threatening. Beth Ann was whisked away to a local hospital for further treatment and observation.

Still noticeably shaken, Summer's parents, Derrick, and her brother hung around to talk.

Summer and Angel still troubled as well eventually emerged from back stage to join them.

Deidra called for photos to be taken. Ted D' Francisco, Summer's stellar photographer lingering onsite snapped a series of pictures.

Summer and Derrick's love was evident in each photograph.

Summer's life was finally full circle. Summer's Bridal Fashions was poised for future success. And she was now engaged to Derrick Hamilton an awe-inspiring Christian minister and business professional.

ABOUT THE AUTHOR

Eddie Johnson is an independent book author and self-publisher. His most recent works in the romance church drama genre are Megan's Fools Paradise, Dating a Single Minister, and Temptation in the Pulpit. And in the poetry genre his works are Reaching For Celestial Heights a collection of religious, and inspirational poems; and The Love of a Mother & Father a condensed selection of holiday and marital anniversary poems.

Throughout Eddie's life he's held jobs assisting others. He worked as a Public Assistance Specialist with the State of Florida for over a decade. Since then he has worked in private sector customer relations and billing related positions in telecommunications and banking. He has a Degree in Business Data Processing. Eddie is a devoted husband and father.

www.ingramcontent.com/pod-product-compliance
Lightning Source LLC
Chambersburg PA
CBHW010936120626
46554CB00007B/2495